Vampire Trouble

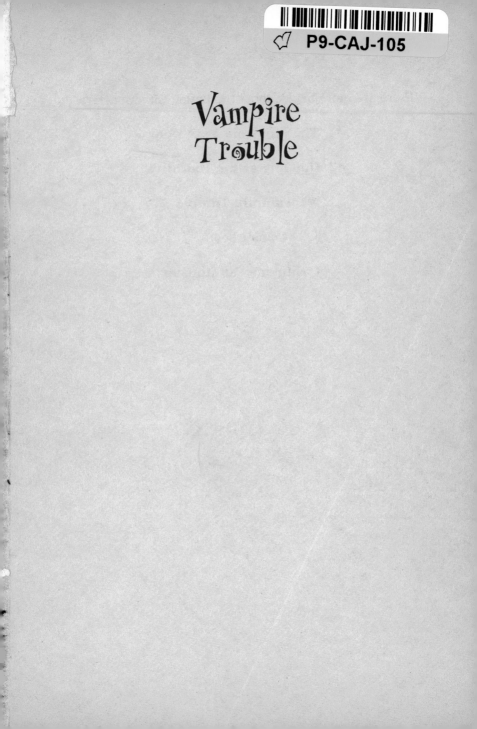

P9-CAJ-105

There are more books about the Bailey City Monsters!

Vampire Trouble

by **Marcia Thornton Jones**
and
Debbie Dadey

illustrated by **John Steven Gurney**

A
LITTLE APPLE
PAPERBACK

SCHOLASTIC INC.
New York   Toronto   London   Auckland   Sydney

ISBN 0-590-10846-8

12 11 10 9 8 7   9/9 0 1 2 3/0

Printed in the U.S.A.   40

First Scholastic printing, April 1998

Book design by Laurie Williams

For Michael and Laura Schafer,
two great neighbors — DD

To Myra Finney and Carolyn Floyd —
two friends who appreciate a good story
when they hear one! — MTJ

Contents

1

Batty

"What was that?" Ben yelled. He ducked as a big black thing swooped over his head.

Ben's sister, Annie, shrugged. "It was only a black bird."

"It looked more like a bat to me," Jane said. Jane was in the fourth grade like Ben, and she was Annie's best friend.

Jane threw the football back to Ben as the sinking sun cast long shadows across Ben and Annie's backyard. Jane, Annie, and Ben were teaching their friend Kilmer Hauntly how to play football.

Kilmer was Ben and Annie's next-door neighbor. Kilmer was in the same grade as Ben and Jane, but Kilmer wasn't a normal fourth-grader. He had just moved to Bailey City from Transylvania. Kilmer was very tall and his hair was cut flat across the top

of his head. In fact, Annie thought Kilmer looked just like Frankenstein's monster.

Ben caught Jane's pass and then threw the ball to Kilmer. "Jane, you wouldn't know a bat if it landed on your nose," Ben said.

"Sure I would," Jane said. "I saw a bunch of them when my family went on vacation to Carlsbad Caverns. Hundreds of bats came out of the cave at night. It was creepy."

"It sounds neat to me," Kilmer said. "I would feel right at home."

"Whatever it was," Annie said, pointing to Kilmer's house, "it landed at Hauntly Manor Inn."

Before Kilmer and his family moved in, the house at 13 Dedman Street had been brand-new. Now, paint peeled from the wood and most of the windows were cracked. Every single tree was dead, and scratchy weeds filled the yard. A loose sign swayed in the wind. It said HAUNTLY MANOR INN, but few people ever dared to spend the night there.

Kilmer took one look at the black thing landing on his porch and tossed the football back to Ben. Kilmer threw the ball so hard, Ben fell backward trying to catch it.

"I have to go," Kilmer shouted. "My grandmother is here!" Kilmer stomped out of Ben's yard, his big heavy shoes making footprints in the damp ground.

"I wonder what Kilmer's grandmother is

like," Annie said after Kilmer disappeared inside Hauntly Manor.

Jane shrugged. Then she spoke so softly Ben and Annie had to step closer to hear. "Since Kilmer's mother looks like a mad scientist and his dad is the spitting image of Count Dracula, it's a sure bet," she whispered, "that Kilmer's grandmother is some kind of monster."

Jane had barely said the word "monster" when the door to Hauntly Manor creaked open and heavy footsteps clomped onto the porch. Kilmer waved to his friends. "Come over and meet my grandmother!" he yelled.

"I hope you're wrong about Kilmer's grandmother," Annie said, "or we may be walking into a monster trap!"

2
Grandma Bloodsucker

Kilmer's grandmother stood at the top of the staircase in Hauntly Manor. She wore a long black dress with flowing sleeves that reached all the way to her bright green fingernails. Most of the older women Annie knew had short gray hair, but Kilmer's grandmother had hair as black as a bat's wings and it hung all the way down her back.

"It is so very nice to meet Kilmer's friends," Kilmer's grandmother said slowly as she glided down the steep stairs. "Please, do call me Madame Hauntly." She spoke with the same Transylvanian accent that the rest of the Hauntlys had, and she wore bloodred lipstick.

Annie, Jane, Ben, and Kilmer followed

Madame Hauntly into the living room. The room was painted deep red and filled with dusty antique furniture. Giant spiderwebs stretched across all corners of the large room.

"It's nice to meet you," Annie said politely. Kilmer's grandmother was so tall that Annie had to tilt her head back to see the woman's pale face. "Has it been a long time since you've seen Kilmer?"

Madame Hauntly put a long bony hand on Annie's shoulder and patted it. Annie could feel how cold Madame Hauntly's hand was even through her sweater. "Yes, it has been too long," Madame Hauntly said. "I have missed my Kilmer dearly. My heart has been saddened to be so far from one of my favorite grandsons. Transylvania has been lonely without him."

"And we have missed you," Boris Hauntly said as he came into the room. Kilmer's dad wore a black cape that swirled around his legs as he walked. He set down a huge tray on a dusty table. "I am sure your long flight was tiring, so I prepared some refreshments for you."

Madame Hauntly looked at the tray. Tall glasses were filled with a thick red drink, and a plate held a pile of green blobs floating in grease.

"It looks delicious," Madame Hauntly told her son. She picked up a glass of the red liquid, took a small sip, and smiled. "Perfect," she said. "Warm, just the way I like it."

"How about some green pickled possum toes?" Boris asked the children. He pointed to the green slimy blobs on a cracked china plate.

Ben shook his head. "No, thanks. I had all the possum toes I could eat earlier today."

Annie gulped and quickly stood up. "We'd better go. You'll want to rest after your long flight."

Madame Hauntly stretched her long arms. "I am tired," she said, "but I feel better now that I am here."

Jane inched toward the front door. "It was nice meeting you. I hope you enjoy visiting Bailey City."

Jane, Annie, and Ben hurried out of Hauntly Manor Inn. They stopped on the creaking porch to catch their breath. A loose shutter banged in the wind and Annie jumped when Kilmer's cat, Sparky, ran past her leg. Sparky's fur stood up in all directions as if she had just been shocked.

"It looks like Sparky had some of that gross-looking red goop to drink," Ben said. "That stuff would make anyone's hair stick up."

"Boris' food gave me the creeps," Annie added. "What was that weird stuff Madame Hauntly drank?"

Ben shrugged. "I don't know, but if you want to see something really strange, look over there."

3
Grandma's Bed

A huge truck pulled to a stop in front of Hauntly Manor Inn. Two men dressed in solid black climbed out. They glanced at the three kids, but they didn't smile. Instead, they hurried to the back of the truck and swung open the heavy doors.

"What do you think they're unloading?" Annie asked.

"Probably furniture," Jane said. "My parents' new bed came in that kind of truck."

The men didn't carry a bed out of the truck. Instead, they each held one end of a long, narrow wooden box. The box was made from dark wood, and a lid covered the top. It was so long, a basketball player could stretch out inside and still have room to wiggle his toes. The moving men slowly carried the box up the cracked sidewalk of Hauntly Manor Inn. The kids moved out of the way and watched from Ben and Annie's backyard.

The door to the inn opened and Madame Hauntly glided out onto the sagging porch. "Thank you for bringing my baggage," she said in her thick Transylvanian accent. "I would not be able to sleep a wink without it!"

Jane shook her head. "What would Kilmer's grandmother have in a box like that?"

Annie smiled. "Most grandmothers bring special treats from home when they visit. I bet that box is full of games, toys, and other surprises for the whole family."

Madame Hauntly moved to the front of the porch. But when she stepped into a patch of sun she frowned, and quickly stepped back into the shadows. She spoke in a low voice to the men. "Please," she told them, "carry it to the conservatory." Kilmer's grandmother disappeared into

Hauntly Manor Inn, leading the way for the two moving men and the long wooden box.

Jane, Ben, and Annie knew all about Boris Hauntly's conservatory. It was an entire room full of clay pots and dirt beds where most people would plant flowers, but Boris wasn't like most gardeners. Instead, he filled his beds with special dirt from Transylvania, and the pots contained dead-looking sticks and plants. It looked like a graveyard for petunias.

"Why would Madame Hauntly want the surprises in a room full of dirt?" Ben whispered.

"Maybe the box is full of special dirt for Boris' garden," Annie suggested.

"That's it!" Jane said, snapping her fingers. She grabbed Annie's and Ben's arms and pulled them behind the bushes in their front yard.

"What's wrong with you?" Ben asked. "You act like you saw a swamp monster."

Jane's eyes were wide. "I think I figured

it out. That box is full of special dirt, and it is a surprise for everyone in Bailey City."

"All right!" Ben yelled. "I love surprises."

"Madame Hauntly didn't even meet us until today," Annie said. "Why would she bring us a surprise?"

"This isn't that kind of surprise," Jane told her. "The surprise I'm talking about spells trouble if anyone finds out. Big trouble."

"Madame Hauntly came to visit Kilmer," Annie said. "She didn't come to cause trouble."

"But don't you know what that box is?" Jane asked.

"Sure," Ben said. "It's a trunk, an old-fashioned suitcase."

Annie nodded. "Madame Hauntly is a grandmother. That means she's old. She's probably had that trunk forever."

Jane nodded. "Forever is exactly what I mean. Don't you get it? That box isn't full of dirt for Boris' garden," she explained. "It's full of dirt for herself."

"Why would Madame Hauntly bring dirt all the way from Transylvania?" Ben asked.

"For the same reason Boris and Hilda did when they first moved here," Jane explained. "Everybody knows vampires sleep in coffins. But not everybody knows that vampires can't sleep without soil from their native country."

"What does all of this have to do with our neighbors?" Annie asked.

"Madame Hauntly's box is really her coffin full of dirt from Transylvania," Jane told her. "And those long dirt piles in the conservatory are beds, but they're not for tulips and daffodils. They're for vampires!"

4
Vampire Visitors

"VAMPIRES?" Annie shrieked. "Are you crazy?"

"Shhh," Jane warned. "We don't want Madame Hauntly to hear us."

Jane peeked over the bushes at Hauntly Manor Inn.

"Jane's right," Ben said.

"You mean you agree with Jane?" Annie asked.

Ben grinned. "I agree we don't want Madame Hauntly to hear because she'll think Jane is nuttier than peanut butter."

Jane narrowed her eyes and curled her fingers into a fist. "I'll make you a deal. You take that back," she said, "and I won't give you a black eye."

Before Ben could answer, Annie tugged on his sleeve. Annie's face had suddenly

gone pale, and she looked ready to cry. "Look who's coming!" she said, pointing to the sidewalk.

Mrs. Jeepers was walking slowly down Dedman Street. Mrs. Jeepers was one of the third-grade teachers at Bailey School. Most of the kids said Mrs. Jeepers was a vampire, and Annie believed them. Annie was glad she wasn't in Mrs. Jeepers' class.

Mrs. Jeepers' long red hair was pulled back with a green ribbon, and Annie could see the green brooch Mrs. Jeepers always wore pinned near her throat. Kids in her class said the pin glowed when Mrs. Jeepers rubbed it, and they were sure the brooch was full of magic.

"What is she doing on Dedman Street?" Ben asked. Ben didn't like Mrs. Jeepers very much, either. She had a habit of catching him when he caused trouble, which happened a lot.

"Remember," Annie whimpered, "Mrs. Jeepers is Kilmer's aunt."

Ben, Annie, and Jane watched as Mrs. Jeepers hurried closer. She glanced toward the bush that the three kids had ducked behind. Annie closed her eyes and Jane held her breath. Mrs. Jeepers took a step in their direction, but just then the door to Hauntly Manor Inn squeaked open.

Kilmer jumped onto the porch with his heavy brown shoes and yelled, "Auntie Jeepers, guess who's here?"

Mrs. Jeepers didn't have to guess because Madame Hauntly moved onto the porch and waved.

"Mother!" Mrs. Jeepers yelled. "I am so glad to see you."

"That was a close call," Annie whispered, watching the third-grade teacher rush up the steps to hug Kilmer's grandmother. "I thought we were in big trouble."

"We are," Jane said.

"No, we're not," Ben argued. "Mrs. Jeepers didn't see us."

"It doesn't matter," Jane said. "If

Madame Hauntly is Mrs. Jeepers' mother, that means trouble for us and for everyone here on Dedman Street."

"The only thing this means is that your brain has turned to dust," Ben said.

"Oh, my gosh, everyone says that Mrs. Jeepers is a vampire," Annie said with a gasp. "If that's true, then her mother must be . . ."

"That's right," Jane said. "Madame Hauntly is a vampire and the vampires are taking over Dedman Street!"

5

Spying on a Vampire

"You must have been taking a nap when they handed out brains." Ben poked Jane in the head. "You haven't lost your marbles — you never had any to begin with!"

"I'm smarter than you," Jane said. "I figured out that Kilmer's grandmother is a monster."

Annie gulped. "Maybe we should all go home and put on turtlenecks," she suggested.

Ben pulled his shirt collar down and stretched his neck out. "Here, little vampires, come and get it!" he yelled.

"Shhh," Annie gasped. "Don't do that. What if Madame Hauntly or Mrs. Jeepers hears you?"

"Or Boris Hauntly," Jane added. "If he's

not Count Dracula's twin brother, then I'm
a box of rocks."

"You look like a block of concrete to
me," Ben sneered. "And shame on both
of you for calling Kilmer's poor sweet
grandma a monster."

"I'm sorry," Annie said. "I'm just scared."

"There's nothing to be scared of," Ben
said. "And I'm going to show you."

"What are you going to do?" Jane asked.

"I'm going to keep an eye on Granny and
see what she does," Ben told her. "I'll see

she's just a regular old lady with weird clothes. Unless you're scared, you'll go with me."

"I'll go," Jane said, pulling her collar up, "because I want to watch you get your neck bitten. Then I'll have proof that you're a real monster, too."

Ben didn't say another word. He headed to the back of Hauntly Manor Inn, where the conservatory was located. Ben hid behind a dead elm tree and peered into the big glass room. Jane and Annie came up behind him. "What's going on?" Annie whispered.

"It looks like they're digging," Ben explained. He pointed to the mounds of dirt in the middle of the conservatory.

"Or burying something," Jane said with a gulp. Mrs. Jeepers, Kilmer, Boris Hauntly, and his wife, Hilda, stood beside the mounds. Dead plants surrounded them. Boris and Mrs. Jeepers each had shovels.

Madame Hauntly led the moving men

into the conservatory and pointed to one of the mounds. The men gently set the huge box down and hurried out of the room.

As soon as the men left, Madame Hauntly got on her knees beside the box and kneeled down. She pressed her lips to the dirt.

"Yuck!" Annie said. "She's kissing dirt."

"Maybe she's eating it," Ben said. "It has to taste better than green pickled possum toes."

"Where's she going?" Annie asked. The three kids watched Madame Hauntly leave the room.

"She's probably going to turn into a bat and fly to the nearest cave," Jane said.

"If she's looking for an empty cave, your head would be perfect," Ben joked.

"Ha-ha." Jane pretended to laugh. "I'll make you a deal. You go jump in the nearest lake and I'll throw you a life preserver . . . a concrete one."

Ben stuck out his tongue at Jane and Jane pushed Ben. Annie was the only one who saw the dark figure approaching them, and Annie didn't notice until it was too late.

6
Dead Darlings

"My darling children," Madame Hauntly said, grabbing Ben and Jane by the shoulders. "I am so glad to see you again. I noticed you watching through the window. Please join us in the conservatory for the festivities."

Ben shook his head quickly. "No, thanks," he said. "We were just leaving."

"Oh, but I insist," Madame Hauntly said, pulling Ben and Jane toward the back of the house.

"Help," Ben squeaked at Annie. "Save me."

Madame Hauntly chuckled. "You Americans are so funny. I love your humor."

"I love living," Ben said. Annie shrugged and followed Ben, Jane, and Madame Hauntly into the darkened conservatory.

Blinds had been lowered throughout the glass room, and hundreds of candles sat in the dirt, casting shadows on Madame Hauntly's face.

"Please be seated," Madame Hauntly said. "We will begin." Ben, Annie, and Jane sat on one of the dirt mounds.

"What are they beginning?" Annie whispered.

"They're going to make us into dead darlings," Ben explained.

Jane punched Ben in the shoulder. "I thought you didn't believe that Madame Hauntly is a vampire."

Ben shrugged. "I don't know what to think."

Kilmer, Boris, Hilda, Mrs. Jeepers, and Madame Hauntly seated themselves on the dirt mounds around the children. "How should we start?" Madame Hauntly asked.

"Tell the one about Great-grandfather Hauntly," Kilmer said.

Madame Hauntly nodded. "Many, many years ago there lived a boy named Edwardo

Hauntly. He grew up strong and handsome, with flaming red hair." Madame Hauntly paused and smiled at Mrs. Jeepers.

"Edwardo learned to be a farmer, a good farmer. He had a beautiful wife and six children. But an evil man lived nearby who called himself Vlad. This evil man tried to steal Edwardo's land and even Edwardo's wife. For a time, Vlad partly succeeded. Edwardo's wife talked Edwardo into leaving the land, but without the land to provide their food, the family soon became hungry. Edwardo sneaked away to fight Vlad.

"The battle went on for six days. Vlad was a fierce fighter, but Edwardo fought for his six children and his wife. Every time Edwardo was near losing, he thought of his hungry children and he fought harder. Finally, on the sixth day, Edwardo won the battle and Vlad agreed to give back Edwardo's land, but only on one condition."

"What condition?" Ben asked.

Madame Hauntly smiled, showing her huge eyeteeth. "Edwardo agreed to only

EDWARDO

farm at night and never appear on his land during the day. Even now, Hauntlys shun the daylight as often as possible, staying in the dark as a tribute to Edwardo and his bravery."

"That's some story," Annie said.

"Tell another one," Kilmer asked his grandmother.

"Is that what you're doing here?" Ben asked. "Telling stories?"

Hilda Hauntly nodded, her wild hair bobbing up and down. "Certainly, what did you think we were going to do?"

Ben gulped. "Oh, nothing."

"Would you like to share a story?" Madame Hauntly asked. "I am sure such nice young people have wonderful stories to share."

Annie smiled, but shook her head. "We'd love to hear more of your stories."

Madame Hauntly patted Annie on the head and started another story.

Annie, Ben, and Jane sat spellbound as Madame Hauntly told tales of long-ago times and ancient relatives. Every story held excitement, adventure, and danger. They were exactly the type of stories Ben loved.

Finally, Madame Hauntly held up her

hand. "Enough stories," she said. "It is time for an old woman to rest."

"No," Ben begged. "Don't quit."

Madame Hauntly smiled and laid down on top of one of the big piles of dirt. She closed her eyes, folded her hands on her chest, and two minutes later she was snoring.

"We'd better leave her alone," Kilmer told the kids. "Grandmother likes to nap during the day. She has more energy when it's dark outside."

Annie shivered when she saw Madame Hauntly's still form. "Thanks for the stories," she said quickly. "We'll leave now."

"Did you see her sleeping in the dirt?" Jane asked later as the kids walked home. "I told you she was a vampire."

"She's a cool lady," Ben said. "I wouldn't care if she were Queen Vampirola."

Annie nodded. "She did tell neat stories. I wish our grandmother would visit and tell fun stories like that. I guess Madame

Hauntly was exhausted after traveling all the way from Transylvania."

"That's because she flew with her own wings," Jane said. "I think Madame Hauntly was that big bat we saw."

"Put a sock in it," Ben said. "I plan to have fun with Madame Hauntly and listen to all her stories. Kilmer said we can go with him tomorrow when he shows his grandmother around Bailey City."

"And if his grandmother bites us on the neck," Jane said, "we can all fly around Bailey City together as bats!"

7

Delicious Treats

The next day, Kilmer and his grandmother weren't ready until the sun sank
low in the evening sky. Ben, Jane, and Annie
climbed the steps to Hauntly Manor. They
took a step back when the door slowly
swung open and Madame Hauntly glided
out onto the porch. She wore a long black
dress that dragged on the ground, and her
lips were covered with deep red lipstick.

"I am looking forward to seeing all the
delicious treats Bailey City has to offer,"
Madame Hauntly told the children.

"We should show your grandmother the
playground," Ben said.

"Why would a grandmother want to see
the playground?" Annie asked.

But Madame Hauntly clapped her hands.
"I would enjoy meeting more of your

friends," she told Kilmer. "The playground is the perfect place."

Kilmer and Madame Hauntly headed down Dedman Street. Madame Hauntly's dress was so long, the kids couldn't see her feet. They could hear Kilmer's heavy shoes hitting the sidewalk, but Madame Hauntly didn't make a sound.

Ben hurried after Kilmer and his grandmother. Annie and Jane followed close behind. They didn't slow down until they reached the Bailey School playground.

Several kids were kicking a soccer ball. A boy named Huey grabbed the soccer ball and ran over to Kilmer. "How about a game of soccer?" he asked.

A girl named Carey nodded. "We need more kids to make a team," she said. Then Carey held out her hand to Madame Hauntly. "My name is Carey," she said. "It's nice to meet you."

When Madame Hauntly licked her lips and smiled, Carey dropped her hand to her side and took a giant step back.

"We can't play," Kilmer explained. "I am showing my grandmother around Bailey City."

"Of course you can play," Madame Hauntly said. "I will rest under the branches of this beautiful oak tree."

Jane pointed to the sky. "The sun is ready to set. There are only a few minutes of light left. We won't be playing long."

The group of kids raced across the playground after the soccer ball, leaving Madame Hauntly in the shadows of the oak tree.

When Kilmer kicked the ball, Madame Hauntly cheered. She yelled for Ben, Jane, and Annie, too.

Finally, Annie told Kilmer, "We'd better go back to your grandmother."

But when the kids looked toward the shadows of the oak tree, Madame Hauntly was nowhere to be seen.

8

Monster Shakes

"Where did she go?" Carey asked.

"She disappeared into thin air!" Annie shrieked.

Kilmer didn't seem worried. He held his hands to his mouth and hollered, "Grandmother? Where did you fly off to?"

High in the oak tree, leaves rustled when Madame Hauntly pulled back a few branches to wave. "I am perched up here," she called down. "It was the perfect place to watch your game."

"Cool," Ben said. "A grandmother that climbs trees!" All the kids raced to the tree to see if Madame Hauntly needed help climbing back down. But by the time they reached the tree, she was already standing on the ground.

"What treat will you show me next?" Madame Hauntly asked.

"Burger Doodle!" Ben yelled. "They have the best Doodlegum Shakes in town!"

Madame Hauntly licked her lips so they glistened. "I would enjoy sipping a drink," she said. "I will buy everyone a shake!"

"We'll have to hurry," Jane said. "It's getting dark."

Madame Hauntly glanced at the darkening sky. The moon was already low on the horizon. "There is nothing to fear from darkness," she told the children. "I have told your parents we may be late. So let us enjoy the night!"

Madame Hauntly glided down the sidewalk with Kilmer leading the way. Before Annie, Jane, and Ben could join them, Carey reached out and grabbed them. "How did she do that?" Carey whispered. "Nobody has climbed that high in the oak tree before."

Annie shrugged. "She probably has one

of those stair climbers at home. My mother has one, but she never uses it."

Carey shook her head so hard, her blond curls bounced. "There is no way she could climb that fast."

"But she had to climb up there," Jane said. "That's the only way to get up in a tree."

"There is another way," Carey said slowly.

"How?" Annie asked.

Carey looked each of them in the eyes before answering. "By flying!"

Annie giggled and Ben laughed out loud. But Jane didn't say a word.

"You have to admit," Carey added, "there is something strange about Kilmer's grandmother."

"Don't be silly," Ben said. "Kilmer's grandmother is the coolest adult I've ever met. She knows how to have fun with kids. She's even going to treat us to Doodlegum Shakes."

"Either that," Carey said slowly, "or she's fattening us up."

"For what?" Annie asked.

"For dinner!" Carey told them. "I think Kilmer's grandmother is a vampire and we're her next meal. I bet instead of going to drive-through windows she goes to fly-throughs!"

Ben laughed so hard, Kilmer heard him and stopped.

"Is there something the matter?" Madame Hauntly called to them.

Carey grabbed Ben's elbow. "Don't go with her," she said. "It may be the last thing you do."

Ben glared at Carey's hand holding his arm. "If you don't let go of me, it WILL be the last thing you do," he told her, shaking his arm free from her grasp. "Besides, you're batty. The only weird thing about Madame Hauntly is that she's being nice to you." With that, Ben ran to catch up with Kilmer and his grandmother.

"We'll see," Carey said as she followed behind Jane and Annie.

Burger Doodle was deserted except for the kids and Madame Hauntly. They all ordered milk shakes and sat in a dark corner. Madame Hauntly closed her eyes and sucked her strawberry shake with loud slurping noises.

Carey pushed her shake away and stared at Kilmer's grandmother before standing up and brushing her blond curls back from her face. "That is the most disgusting thing I ever heard," she said out loud.

Jane and Annie gasped when Madame Hauntly slowly opened her eyes and stared straight at Carey.

Ben just grinned. "Then you haven't heard the noises I can make," he said with a laugh. "I know how to make sounds that would make you want to crawl in a cave and not come out for ten years," he told Carey. "Do you want me to prove it?"

Carey glared at Ben. "You are as strange as Kilmer and his grandmother," she said. "I can't decide who is the worst. You're all monsters, and I plan to do something about it!"

9
Carey Strikes Again

After Carey stormed out of Burger Doodle, Jane leaned over to Madame Hauntly.

"We're sorry," Jane said to Madame Hauntly.

"Carey can be very rude," Annie added.

Madame Hauntly smiled at Kilmer and his friends. "I have learned not to fear what people say," she told them. "They cannot hurt me with their words."

Ben shrugged. "She's gone now. She won't bother us anymore." But Ben was wrong. He forgot one thing. Carey could be very stubborn.

The next morning, Carey marched down Dedman Street. She stopped right in front of Hauntly Manor Inn and jabbed a big sign into the ground.

Ben and Annie watched from the window of their house. "What is she doing?" Annie asked.

Ben headed for the door. "There's only one way to find out."

Jane was already standing in Ben and Annie's front yard. Ben and Annie hurried to join her so they could see Carey's sign. In big black letters Carey had written BEWARE OF VAMPIRES. A picture of fangs dripping blood was drawn below the words.

"Is she crazy?" Ben asked. "She can't just go sticking signs in people's yards."

"Carey is used to doing whatever she wants to," Annie said.

"That's true," Jane said. Carey's dad was the president of Bailey City Bank, and Jane never liked the way Carey always got her way.

"We can't let the Hauntlys see the sign," Annie said. "It will hurt their feelings."

Ben checked his watch. "We don't have to worry about Kilmer's folks. They never come outside much during the day. We'll just wait until Carey goes away, and then we'll take down her sign," he said.

Ben was right. Kilmer's parents didn't come outside, but Kilmer did. "What is going on?" he asked Ben.

Ben shrugged. "Carey is just being a wet turnip."

"I'm sorry," Annie said. "I hope she didn't hurt your feelings."

Kilmer shook his head. "Remember, my grandmother said to not let what people say hurt you."

"Don't worry about it," Ben said as Kilmer headed back to Hauntly Manor. "I'm sure she'll go home soon."

But Carey didn't go away. Instead, she put something around her neck. Then she picked up another sign and started marching up the sidewalk, straight toward Ben, Jane, and Annie. With each step she chanted three words. "GO HOME, VAMPIRES!"

Carey stomped right past Ben, Annie, and Jane. When she did, the three kids nearly choked.

"What is that smell?" Annie asked, holding her nose.

"I always knew girls were stinky," Ben said. "But this is worse than a sewer!"

Jane ignored Ben and pointed to Carey. "That smell isn't Carey," she explained. "It's her necklace."

"What is it made from?" Ben asked. "Wet dog fur?"

"No," Jane said. "It's made from garlic to keep away vampires."

The three kids watched Carey go all the way down to the corner of Dedman Street. Then she turned around and headed back. By the time she was halfway down the street, three other neighbors had come outside to watch.

"This has gone too far," Ben said, stomping his foot. "The rest of the neighborhood is starting to notice. We have to stop her."

"What if everybody in the neighborhood joins in with Carey?" Jane asked.

"That's exactly why we should stop her," Annie said. "Carey is being rude to the Hauntlys."

"This is our chance to make sure Carey doesn't get her way for once," Ben added.

"We've got to do something," Annie said. "After all, Kilmer's grandmother did treat us to Doodlegum Shakes."

"And she tells great stories," Ben said.

"She's the nicest adult on Dedman Street," Annie said.

"All right," Jane said. "How can we stop Carey?"

Ben grinned. "I'm glad you asked," he said. "I have the perfect plan!"

10
Plan V

Carey marched up and down Dedman Street until the sun climbed high in the sky. Then her mother called her home for lunch. Before leaving, Carey yelled, "I'll be back first thing tomorrow."

"She's finally gone home," Ben told Jane and Annie. "It's time to put Plan V into action."

"What is Plan V?" Annie asked.

Ben smiled. "Plan Vampire, just like we talked about. As in, save our friendly neighborhood vampires from the real bloodsucker named Carey."

"I hope this isn't being too mean," Annie said when Ben stopped talking.

Jane shook her head. "Carey deserves to be put in her place for once. She's always acting like she's better than everyone else.

61

She didn't have to be so rude to Madame Hauntly."

"Maybe this will teach her a lesson," Ben said. "Besides, if we don't do something, she's not going to let poor Madame Hauntly alone."

"All right," Annie said. "Let's do it. Commence Plan V." Annie took a jar of green goop, a bag of funny pajamas that her aunt May had given her for a joke, and a box of hair rollers that she'd borrowed from her mother. She headed over to Carey's house.

"Hi, Carey!" Annie said with a smile. "Can you play?"

Carey didn't get a lot of people coming over to her house, so Annie was invited in right away. Annie played for quite a while, and when she left she was empty-handed.

"I feel very guilty," Annie said when she got home. "Carey really needs a friend."

"If she wasn't so mean, she'd have lots of friends," Ben pointed out.

Jane patted Annie's shoulder. "You can be her friend tomorrow, after Plan V works."

"All right," Annie said with a sigh. "I told her to be ready at seven tonight. She said she was looking forward to a total beauty makeover."

Ben nodded, then threw on his vampire cape, while Annie and Jane painted their faces white and drew on bloody fangs.

Next, Jane made phone call after phone call and tried to talk in a very grown-up voice. "Yes." She nodded after talking for a while. "It will be a very newsworthy event."

11

Meanest Monster of All

As the sun faded from the sky, the three kids emerged from Ben's house looking like a kid's worst nightmare.

First, the kids pulled up the BEWARE OF VAMPIRES sign from the ground at Hauntly Manor Inn. They walked down the block to Olympus Lane and sank the sign into the ground in front of a huge white mansion. Annie giggled. "I hope Carey likes her new lawn ornament." The kids didn't have to wait long to find out, because Carey flew out of the house in a rage.

"What are you doing?" Carey yelled.

Annie and Jane shouted, "Go home, vampires! Go home, vampires!"

Ben couldn't shout. After looking at Carey, he couldn't do anything but laugh.

Ben bent over laughing and pointed at Carey.

Carey did make a funny picture with her face covered in green goop. Her hair was in bright green and pink hair rollers. She wore pajamas with feet in them that made her look like a big rabbit. The pajamas even had a carrot dangling on the side.

Before Carey could yell again, the real excitement began. A television van pulled up and a reporter from WMTJ hopped out. A cameraman pointed his camera right at Carey and the kids. Lots of people came out of their houses to see what was going on. Even the Hauntlys came up behind Ben.

"We've heard a rumor of monsters being seen in the neighborhood," the reporter said, sticking a microphone in Ben's face. "Do you have any comment?" he asked.

Ben smiled and grabbed the microphone.

"Oh, no," Jane moaned. "Here goes the biggest show-off in the history of Bailey City."

"Yes," Ben said, ignoring Jane. "It's true. There really is a monster in the neighborhood."

Annie held her breath and looked at Madame Hauntly.

"And right now," Ben continued, "I would like to introduce you to the biggest monster ever."

Carey glared at Madame Hauntly. But Ben didn't shove the microphone in front of Madame Hauntly, he held it in front of Carey. "I'd like all of Bailey City to meet the meanest monster of all — Carey in her pj's!"

"Awww!" Carey screamed and put her hands in front of her face. She turned and ran back into her big white house, with the little bunny tail flapping behind her.

Kilmer and Madame Hauntly laughed. "Ben," Madame Hauntly said, "you are a wonderful young man to stand up for an old bat like me."

Ben shrugged. "People on Dedman Street have to stick up for one another."

Madame Hauntly patted Ben on the shoulder. "You have made me feel so welcome," she said. "Perhaps I should consider making Dedman Street my permanent home."

"That would be neat," Ben said. "Then I could brag to all my friends about the cool grandma I have next door to me."

Madame Hauntly smiled, showing her pointy eyeteeth before floating off toward

Hauntly Manor Inn along with the rest of the Hauntlys.

"Did she say she might stay here?" Jane asked.

Annie smacked herself in the head. "Oh, no," she said. "What have we done? Dedman Street is getting a little too full of monsters."

Ben shrugged again and smiled. "Look at it this way. As long as they're on our side, we have nothing to worry about."